Pamela Duncan Edwards • Illustrated by Sue Porter

McGillycuddy
Could!

KATHERINE TEGEN BOOKS
An Imprint of HarperCollins*Publishers*

McGillycuddy Could!
Text copyright © 2005 by Pamela Duncan Edwards
Illustrations copyright © 2005 by Sue Porter
Manufactured in China by South China Printing Company Ltd.
All rights reserved.
www.harperchildrens.com

Library of Congress Cataloging-in-Publication Data
Edwards, Pamela Duncan.
    McGillycuddy could! / Pamela Duncan Edwards ; illustrated by Sue Porter.— 1st ed.
        p.   cm.
    Summary: Although McGillycuddy the kangaroo cannot produce wool or milk or lay eggs,
the other animals learn that kangaroos can bring special skills to the farm.
    ISBN 0-06-029001-3 — ISBN 0-06-029002-1 (lib. bdg.)
    [1. Kangaroos—Fiction. 2. Domestic animals—Fiction. 3. Animals—Fiction.
4. Farm life—Fiction.] I. Porter, Sue, ill. II. Title.
PZ7.E26365Mc 2005   2003024483
[E]—dc22   CIP
                                                                                  AC

Typography by Jeanne L. Hogle
1 2 3 4 5 6 7 8 9 10

First Edition

For Nicholas Lawley, who will always say "I'LL TRY," with love

—P.D.E.

For Max, Freya, and Reuben, with love

—S.P.

"What's that coming through the gate?" mooed the cow.

"Where did it come from?" baa-ed the sheep.

"I've never seen anything like it," clucked the hen.

"It's not from around here, that's for sure," crowed the rooster.

"What are you?" asked the cow.

"I'm McGillycuddy," said McGillycuddy. "I've just moved in."

"We've never seen a McGillycuddy before," said the cow.

"What do McGillycuddys do?"

"They **hop**," said McGillycuddy.

"Huh!" said the cow. "That's all? I make milk for the farmer to drink. Can you make milk?"

"I can try," said McGillycuddy.

So McGillycuddy tried. But...

McGillycuddy couldn't!

"You can't make milk," said the sheep. "So what DO McGillycuddys do?"

"They **jump**," said McGillycuddy.

"Huh!" said the sheep. "That's all? I grow wool
to keep the farmer warm. Can you do that?"

"I can try," said McGillycuddy.

So McGillycuddy tried. But . . .

McGillycuddy couldn't!

"You can't make milk and you can't grow wool,"
said the hen. "So what DO McGillycuddys do?"
"They **bounce**," said McGillycuddy.

"Huh!" said the hen. "That's all? I lay eggs for the farmer to eat. Can you do that?"

"I can try," said McGillycuddy.

So McGillycuddy tried. But . . .

McGillycuddy couldn't!

"You can't make milk and you can't grow wool and you can't lay eggs," crowed the rooster. "So what DO McGillycuddys do?"

"They **kick**," said McGillycuddy.

"Huh!" said the rooster. "That's all? I cry
'Cock-a-doodle-doo' to wake the farmer in the
morning. Can you do that?"

"I can try," said McGillycuddy.

So McGillycuddy tried. But . . .

McGillycuddy couldn't!

"I don't think McGillycuddys can do very much,"
said McGillycuddy sadly.

"A-hunting I will go," sang a scary voice.

"I want a fat duckling for my supper!"

"Oh! Oh!" quacked the duck. "Who can save me from the fox?"

"I can't," mooed the cow.

"I can't," baa-ed the sheep.

"I can't," clucked the hen.

"I can't," crowed the rooster. But . . .

"I can!" shouted McGillycuddy.
And McGillycuddy could.

Hop!

Jump!

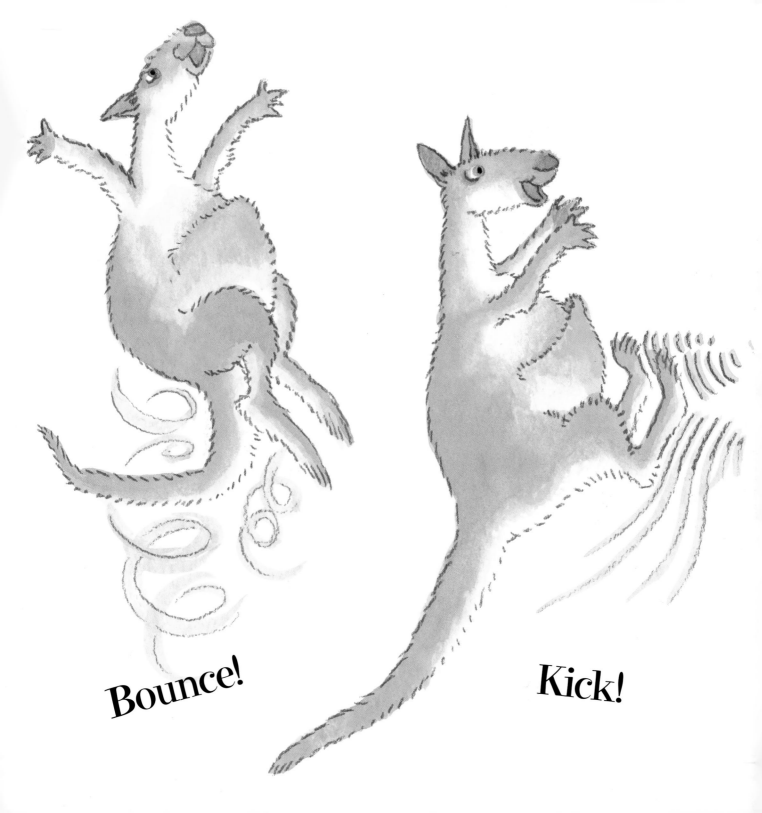

Bounce!

Kick!

Because that's what McGillycuddys do!